W9-AQV-050

MY BIG DUMB INVISIBLE DRAGON

Sounds True
Boulder, CO 80306

Text © 2019 by Angie Lucas
Illustrations © by 2019 Birgitta Sif

Published 2019

Book design by Ranée Kahler
Cover image by Birgitta Sif

Printed in South Korea

Library of Congress Cataloging-in-Publication Data

Names: Lucas, Angie, author. | Sif, Birgitta, illustrator.
Title: My big, dumb, invisible dragon / by Angie Lucas ; illustrated by
  Birgitta Sif.
Description: Boulder, CO : Sounds True, 2019. | Summary: The day a young boy
  loses his mother, an invisible dragon swoops in and stays with him,
  weighing him down day and night until, at last, their relationship
  changes.
Identifiers: LCCN 2018047849 (print) | LCCN 2018052710 (ebook) |
  ISBN 9781683642435 (ebook) | ISBN 9781683641841 (hardcover)
Subjects: | CYAC: Grief—Fiction. | Dragons—Fiction.
Classification: LCC PZ7.1.L7895 (ebook) | LCC PZ7.1.L7895 My 2019 (print) |
  DDC [E]—dc23
LC record available at https://lccn.loc.gov/2018047849

10 9 8 7 6 5 4 3 2 1

For Holland, Mackenzie, and Shauna—
and all who carry them in their hearts.
—AL

For all those who have loved.
—BS

MY BIG DUMB INVISIBLE DRAGON

WRITTEN BY
ANGIE LUCAS

ILLUSTRATED BY
BIRGITTA SIF

Have you ever seen an invisible dragon?
Neither had I.

But one day last May, a giant one swooped in
and landed on my head—right on top of my head!

It was the day Ollie's mom came to get us from Turtle Hill Park,
instead of my mom. She had a funny look on her face,
and she opened her mouth three times
before any words came out.

I don't know if the dragon rode to the park with Ollie's mom,
or if he was already there, hiding in the trees.

All I know is I didn't see him coming.
And once he was there, he would *not* go away.

Dad and I had to get used to making dinner
without Mom there.

We had to get used to how quiet it was in the car
without her singing along to the radio.

We had to get used to movie night without her famous peanut brittle popcorn. But that big, dumb dragon didn't even notice. He moved right in and made himself at home.

He curled up on my chest every night when I was
going to sleep. I swear, he must have weighed a ton!
He made it super hard to get out of bed in the morning.

At school, he cast a ginormous shadow that followed me everywhere.

And if you think it was easy to stand up straight
with a dragon on my head, let me tell you—it wasn't.

I think he's the reason some kids
didn't talk to me as much anymore.

Some days, I ignored him.

I pretended he wasn't there at all.

I played hard and laughed like crazy—even louder and crazier than before.
But that didn't make him leave.

Other days, I got angry. You can't believe how mad I got!
I yelled and shouted. At him. At everyone.

What did that dragon do? He put on his headphones and tuned me out.

There were also days when I'd reach up and pull his big, heavy wings around me. I would curl up like a caterpillar and hide away for hours. It wasn't *always* so bad to have him around.

Still, almost every day, I tried to make a deal with him. "If you'll just
get lost, I'll never say a bad word ever again," I told him. I thought maybe
if he left, things could go back to the way they were. But he didn't seem
to care what *I* wanted. Not one bit.

Then one day, when the sky was filled with
cotton-candy clouds, Ollie invited me back to the park.

I made myself roll and cartwheel and
race down Turtle Hill, just like before.

I ran so blazing fast that my hair stood straight up
like uncooked spaghetti, which made Ollie giggle.

Then something happened that I wasn't expecting at all—
for the first time in months, I forgot all about my dragon.

When we ran out of breath, we flopped down on the grass
and took turns spotting shapes in the clouds.

"I see a giant octopus," I said.

"Does that look like a chicken to you?" Ollie asked.

"There's a pig! Or is that a bear?" I asked.

"That one kind of looks like a dinosaur," Ollie said.

"Actually, I'm pretty sure it's a dragon."

I don't know what that dragon saw up there in the clouds, but after that day, he started soaring even higher and staying away longer. He often disappeared during gym and recess. Sometimes he'd miss a whole soccer game.

Once he was gone for an entire weekend!

But he came back, just in time for my birthday party.

I tried all of my tricks to make him go away. *Skedaddle! Vamoose!*

What do you think he did?

He put on a rainbow-striped cone hat and stayed for the party.
I finally just gave him a piece of my birthday cake.

That night as I waited for sleep—

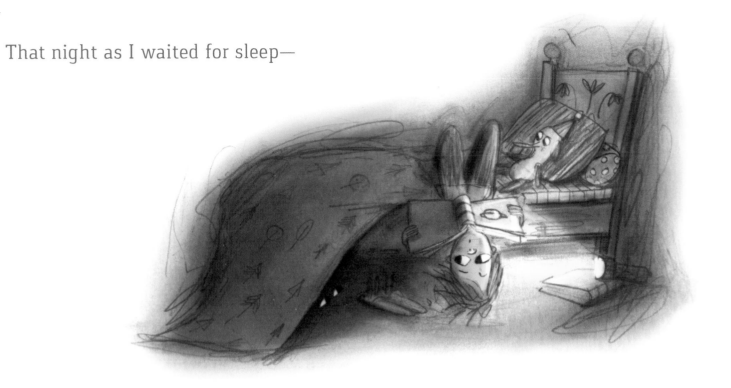

which can take awhile when there's a big, dumb dragon in your bed—

I realized something . . .

My dragon didn't feel as heavy as he did back when I was six.
I guess my birthday wish came a little bit true.

Hey, remember when I asked if you've ever seen
an invisible dragon? That was a silly question.
You can never see one by looking straight at it.

You have to look at the person underneath.